W9-BNV-157

SECRET of the HAUNTED CHIMNEY

Written by Adrian Robert

Illustrated by Irene Trivas

Troll Associates

Library of Congress Cataloging in Publication Data

Robert, Adrian.
    Secret of the haunted chimney.

    Summary: Brian and his brother try to discover the
source of the mysterious sounds coming from their
chimney.
    1. Children's stories, American. [1. Mystery and
detective stories] I. Trivas, Irene, ill. II. Title.
PZ7.R5385Sc   1985   [Fic]   84-8763
ISBN 0-8167-0408-2 (lib. bdg.)
ISBN 0-8167-0409-0 (pbk.)

Copyright © 1985 by Troll Associates
All rights reserved. No part of this book may be used or
reproduced in any manner whatsoever without written permission
from the publisher.
Printed in the United States of America.

10   9   8   7   6   5   4   3

SECRET of the HAUNTED CHIMNEY

One dark night in early spring, Brian
looked out the window. Outside, the wind
whistled. Tree branches tapped on the
window panes.

Only Rick and Sally were home with Brian. Their mother and father were out seeing a movie.

Brian was trying to add 28 and 34. But his mind kept returning to the ghost story Stuffy Craddock had told him that day at recess.

"It's a good night for ghosts," said Brian
aloud.

Sally's eyes got big. Sally was Brian's little
sister. She loved to hear about ghosts and
witches.

Rick, their oldest brother, went to high
school. He was trying to do *his* homework.

Sally climbed on the arm of Rick's chair.
"Tell me a ghost story," she said.

"Oh, no," Rick said. "You'll get scared.
Then you won't want to go to bed."

"No, I won't!" Sally said. I don't *really*
get scared, she thought. "Ghost stories are
fun!"

Brian lay flat on the floor beneath the
lamp. Sally knelt beside him.

"Don't bother me," Brian said. He didn't
look up.

Sally looked at Brian. She looked at Rick.
They were always busy.

Without warning, Sally grabbed Brian's homework paper. He let out a yell.

"Give me my homework!" Brian shouted.

Sally shook her head. "Tell me a ghost story! *Then* I'll give it back!"

Rick frowned at them, but Brian didn't care. He was *mad*.

"All right!" he said. "I'll tell you about the ghost at the Craddock farm."

He turned out the lamp. Now there was only the small light by Rick's chair. Moonlight made the trees look like goblins. Sally shivered.

"Better not," Rick warned. Brian didn't listen.

"Stuffy's grandpa lived on a very old farm," he said. "Once when he was a boy he spent the night there alone. In the middle of the night, *something* came down the chimney."

Sally's eyes opened wide. "What was it?"
she asked.

"Stuffy's grandpa didn't know," said
Brian. "But he heard it rustle. He heard it
moan. In the morning he climbed on the roof
and looked. There was nothing in the
chimney! But it came back that night and
every night that spring. Stuffy's grandfather
says the only explanation was that the noise
was a *ghost*."

Sally started to whimper. "I don't want to go to bed," she cried.

"I knew this would happen," Rick said, closing his book. "Sally, there aren't any ghosts, especially not in new houses like ours. Go get ready for bed. Brian, you finish your homework in your room."

Scratttchh. It was the softest of sounds. But everyone froze. The sound was coming from *the chimney!*

Scratttchh. The sound came again.

Rick walked over and put on the lamp Brian had turned out. He went to the fireplace and knocked on the chimney wall.

"Anybody in there?" he asked.

Silence.

"You see?" Rick said. "It was probably just the sound of the tree branches." He looked at Brian. He looked at Sally, who was too scared to cry.

"Tell you what," said Rick. "Sally can stay up half an hour longer. We'll build a fire and toast marshmallows. I'll play my guitar and we can sing."

Brian liked to hear Rick sing. Rick played
the guitar well. Sometimes he played and
sang with his own band. Sally liked to toast
marshmallows. She liked it so much she
almost forgot she was afraid.

"Sally can get the marshmallows," Rick said. "Brian can get the sticks. I'll go for wood."

The kitchen was bright and cheerful.
Sally didn't mind going there alone. Rick
went out the back door. Left alone in the
room, Brian went to the cupboard in the
fireplace wall. That was where Dad kept
sticks for toasting marshmallows.

S c r a t t t c h h h. There it was again—
the same sound, only louder and much closer.
It was just on the other side of the fireplace
wall. Just inside the chimney.

Then Brian heard another small sound. It
sounded like somebody trapped in a very
small space, scratching hard to get out. The
skin on his neck prickled. He was glad Sally
wasn't there. But he wished Rick *was*.

Sally came in from the kitchen. Rick came in with an armful of wood.

"Open the damper, will you, Brian?" he said.

The damper was a little door in the fireplace ceiling. It let the smoke out. It kept rain and snow and cold from coming in. It was Brian's job to open the damper before a fire was built. It was his job to close the damper when the fire was all burnt out. Dad had taught him how. Brian was proud to be in charge of the damper. But he didn't really want to go near it now. Only he didn't want Rick and Sally to know that.

"There are no ghosts," he reminded himself, "and *never* in new houses."

Brian took hold of the handle. He started turning it to the right as he always did.

The handle wouldn't turn!

Maybe he was turning it the wrong way. He tried turning the handle to the left. It wouldn't go that way, either.

"Hurry up," Rick said. He still had the load of wood in his arms.

Brian took a deep breath. He used both hands. The handle moved a tiny bit.

E-e-e-e-e!

Rick dropped the logs. Sally jumped back. Brian quickly let go of the handle.

Something was inside the chimney. Just on the other side of the damper door!

E-e-e-e-e! The cry came again.

"It *is* a ghost," Sally cried. She flung herself at Brian and held him tight.

Rick knocked on the chimney. The sounds stopped. He tried the damper handle. The sounds started again.

"I'm going outside to have a look," said Rick a bit nervously.

"Me too," Brian and Sally said together.

Rick shook his head. "Brian can come. Sally can put on all the lights and watch us through the window."

Rick and Brian put on their jackets. They each took a flashlight. Then they went out to the yard and turned their lights toward the chimney. They couldn't spot anything. Nothing was creeping on the roof...or down the chimney...or in the trees.

The ground was muddy. Brian could hear it squish. He turned the flashlight toward his shoes.

His skin prickled again. His fingers clutched Rick's arm.

"What's the matter?" Rick asked. He looked at Brian. Then he looked at the ground.

Footprints! Footprints leading to the chimney—footprints like a man's, but very, very small. They looked like the feet of a tiny man who could fit into a chimney—or a small *ghost*.

Rick stared at the footprints, then took
hold of Brian's hand. "Where are we going?"
Brian asked. He had to run to keep up.

"To find our ghost," said Rick. "We won't
tell Sally what we saw. Understand?"

Brian nodded. They wiped their feet on
the doormat and went inside. Rick took his
flashlight to the fireplace. He bent over and
looked up at the damper. He motioned for
Brian to look, too.

The damper door was open a tiny crack—
just enough to get a finger through.

"Just keep your hands away from there,"
said Rick.

"Aim your flashlight at the crack. Take
the biggest marshmallow stick and poke it up
through the opening. Keep poking even if it
won't go far at first. I'm going outside to
watch the roof."

Brian did just what Rick had told him. At first the stick wouldn't go far at all. Then he heard the scratching sounds, loud and close at first. Then they grew fainter, as if something was moving away.

But the moaning was still there. *E-e-e-e-e-e.* It sounded lonely and scared.

Suddenly, Rick came in, grinning. "I think that damper door will open now," he said. "Something's still inside, Sally, but it won't hurt you. Turn the handle just a little way, Brian—and very slowly."

Brian turned it with extreme care. Rick held the flashlight steady. Sally crept closer. Then she jumped. There were masked faces—*three* of them. Everyone started to smile.

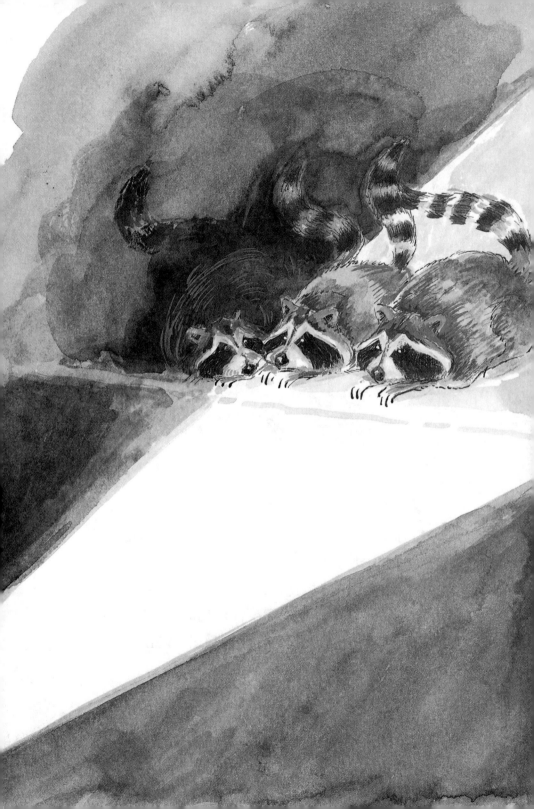

"They won't hurt you, Sally," said Brian.
"They're just babies."

Rick nodded. "There are your ghosts," he
said. "Baby raccoons. Do you know why you
couldn't open the damper, Brian? A mother
raccoon was sleeping on it."

"Where is she now?" asked Sally.

"On the roof," said Rick. "Waiting for us
to let her family alone."

Rick wrapped Sally in a blanket and
carried her outside to see. Brian ran beside
them. Just then the moon came out from
behind the clouds. Tight against the chimney
sat the beautiful mother raccoon.

Brian didn't turn the flashlight on her. He didn't want to scare her away. Our ghosts were afraid of *us*, he thought. We won't do anything more to frighten them. And I won't try to open the damper again. Not till I know the family's grown and gone.

Brian went back inside. Carefully he closed the damper. Inside the chimney, the baby raccoons chirped and rustled and finally went to sleep.

"In the morning," said Brian, "we'll put food outside for their mother to give them. You can help me, Sally. We'll give them water, too. Raccoons need lots of water. They like to put their food in it. I learned that in school."

I learned something else tonight, too, he thought. Tomorrow I'll tell Stuffy what the ghosts in his grandpa's chimney really were—RACCOONS!